Lisa's Letter

by Michael Rosen

Illustrated by Tony Ross

Dear Jo

It's really late and I should be in bed but Mum said it was OK for me to stay up and write to you.
I'll tell you what's happening.

Izzy is scribbling on his T-shirt.

3

Eddie is playing with a ball in the bathroom.

Norma is singing along with the music on the radio.

5

Jack is skateboarding
in his bedroom.

Dad is on his exercise bike.

7

Mum is reading.

And I'm writing to you.

Now Izzy is scribbling on Eddie's ball,

Eddie is singing along
with Norma's radio,

Norma is jumping on Jack's skateboard,

Jack is on Dad's
exercise bike,

13

Dad is reading Mum's book,

and Mum is telling me to stop writing this letter.

Goodbye

Love from
Lisa

Ring Sally

NORMA'S NOTEBOOK

By Michael Rosen   Illustrated by Tony Ross

Ring Sally
Put up poster

Ring Sally
Put up poster
Ring Claire

~~Ring Sally~~
~~Put up poster~~
~~Ring Claire~~
Have tea

4

Ring Sally
Put up poster
Ring Claire
Have tea
Ring Helen

Ring Sally
Put up poster
Ring Claire
Have tea
Ring Helen
Have more tea

Ring Sally
Put up poster
Ring Claire
Have tea
Ring Helen
Have more tea
Ring Katie

Ring Sally
Put up poster
Ring Claire
Have tea
Ring Helen
Have more tea
Ring Katie
Read book

Ring Sally
Put up poster
Ring Claire
Have tea
Ring Helen
Have more tea
Ring Katie
Read book
Ring Emma

9

Ring Sally
Put up poster
Ring Claire
Have tea
Ring Helen
Have more tea
Ring Katie
Read book
Ring Emma
Have drink

Ring Sally
Put up poster
Ring Claire
Have tea
Ring Helen
Have more tea
Ring Katie
Read book
Ring Emma
Have drink
Ring Lee

Ring Sally
Put up poster
Ring Claire
Have tea
Ring Helen
Have more tea
Ring Katie
Read book
Ring Emma
Have drink
Ring Lee
Tease Lisa

Ring Sally
Put up poster
Ring Claire
Have tea
Ring Helen
Have more tea
Ring Katie
Read book
Ring Emma
Have drink
Ring Lee
Tease Lisa
Ring Becky

13

~~Ring Sally~~
~~Put up poster~~
~~Ring Claire~~
~~Have tea~~
~~Ring Helen~~
~~Have more tea~~
~~Ring Katie~~
~~Read book~~
~~Ring Emma~~
~~Have drink~~
~~Ring Lee~~
~~Tease Lisa~~
~~Ring Becky~~
Squeeze Izzy

Ring Sally
Put up poster
Ring Claire
Have tea
Ring Helen
Have more tea
Ring Katie
Read book
Ring Emma
Have drink
Ring Lee
Tease Lisa
Ring Becky
Squeeze Izzy
Ring Kim

Ring Sally
Put up poster
Ring Claire
Have tea
Ring Helen
Have more tea
Ring Katie
Read book
Ring Emma
Have drink
Ring Lee
Tease Lisa
Ring Becky
Squeeze Izzy
Ring Kim
Sleep